WILD WEST
WILLY

as told by
Daniel Postgate

PictureLions
An Imprint of HarperCollins*Publishers*

To Snakey Jake Malone

First published in hardback in Great Britain by HarperCollins Publishers Ltd in 1999
First published in Picture Lions in 2000

1 3 5 7 9 10 8 6 4 2
ISBN: 0 00 664671 9

Picture Lions is an imprint of the Children's Division,
part of HarperCollins Publishers Ltd.

Text and illustrations copyright © Daniel Postgate 1999
The author/illustrator asserts the moral right to be identified as the author/illustrator of the work.

Printed and bound in Singapore by Imago.

Once upon a time, way out
in the wild, wild West,
there stood a brand new town.
It was so new that it didn't
even have a name.

That town was full of the nicest, happiest folk you could ever hope to meet...

…until the day Big Bad Bob Bear
and his boys arrived.
"What's this town called?" he asked.
"It doesn't have a name sir,"
said a goat.
"It does now," said
Bob, "It's called
'Bad Bob Town'."

Big Bad Bob and his boys helped
themselves to whatever they
fancied from the local store...

Then they had a party which went on way after bedtime and kept everyone awake *almost all night.*

The townsfolk were worried.
"This won't do," they said and
sent a letter to the nearest town
by Badger Express.

This is what it said:

BAD BOB HAS
TAKEN OVER
OUR TOWN
PLEASE SEND
HELP RIGHTAWAY.
LOVE FROM
THE TOWN WITH NO
NAME YET X X X

Next morning, Mexican Chicken
rode into town.

"Okay Big Bad Bob, it's time to go," ordered the Chicken.

"Mexican Chicken!"
barked Big Bad
Bob's fox. "My
favourite!"
And he chased
that Chicken right
out of town.

"You'll have to do better than that!" laughed Big Bad Bob, and to teach the townsfolk a lesson, he made them all do lots of horrible chores for him.

"I hope someone else comes to help us soon," they whispered.

On the very next train someone did come.
Elephant George.

"I've wrestled alligators, I've sat on hippos
and I've charged rhinoceroses," he boasted,
"so I'm not scared of this Big Bad Bob Bear.
Where is he?"

"Bob couldn't come," squeaked a little mouse. "So he sent me along instead."

Of course, everybody knows elephants are *terrified* of mice, even Elephant George.

"WAAAAAA!"

he roared, and stampeded
right out of town.

After Elephant George came lots of others who thought they could drive Big Bad Bob out of town. There was...

Big Chief Sitting Duck

The Wild Cat Kid

Randolph the Red Racoon

and even...

Spiky Sam

But Big Bad Bob and his boys scared them all away.

The desperate townsfolk secretly met
in the one place Big Bad Bob would
never go – the school.
"How are we going to get rid of him?"
they all asked.

Then the smelliest, dirtiest, scruffiest
dog in the whole town raised his paw
and said, "I'll do it."
His name was Wild West Willy.

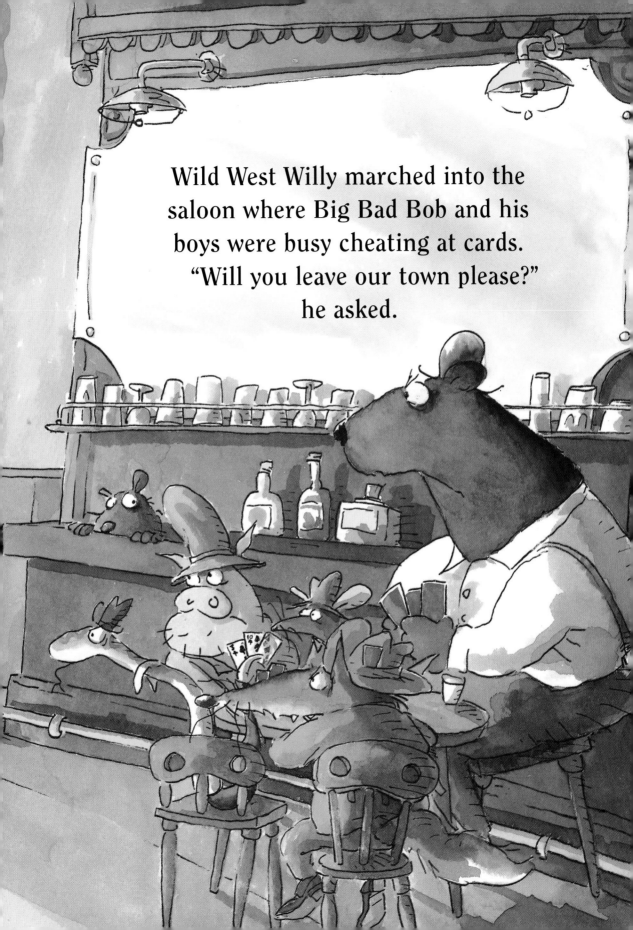

Wild West Willy marched into the saloon where Big Bad Bob and his boys were busy cheating at cards. "Will you leave our town please?" he asked.

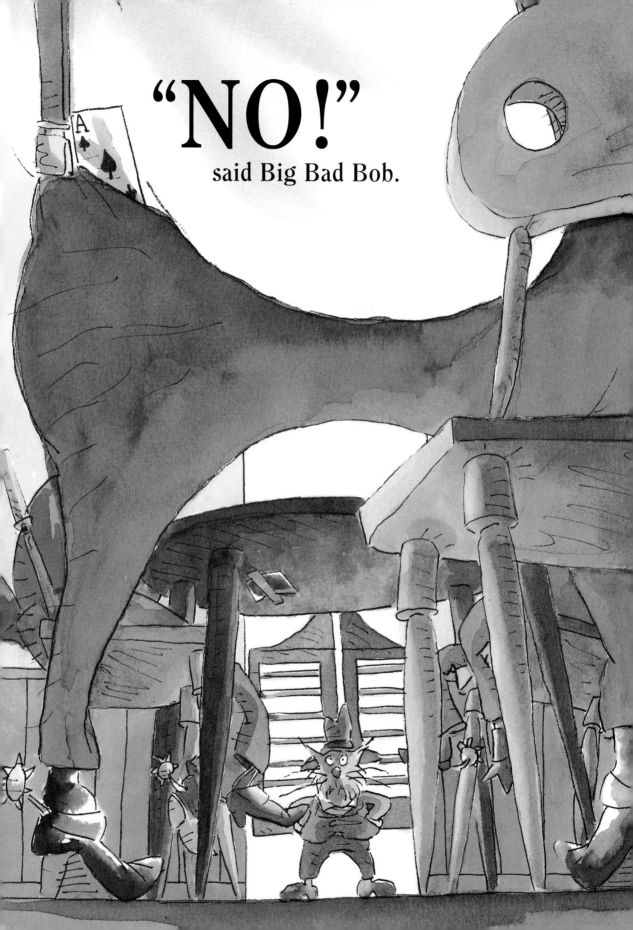

"Well, you asked for it,"
said Wild West Willy, and he gave
himself a good scratching.

"FLEAS!"

cried Big Bad Bob
and his boys. They
danced and scratched
and jumped about.

And jumped and scratched
and danced themselves
right out of town.

"Hooray for Wild West Willy!"
yelled the townsfolk.
And they tossed him high
into the air.

Then they scrubbed him down...

and dressed him up.

And *then* they made him Mayor of... of...